GLUE FINGERS

Books by Matt Christopher

GLUE FINGERS

Matt Christopher

Illustrated by Jim Venable

Little, Brown and Company

BOSTON   TORONTO

FIRST EDITION

T 04/75

Library of Congress Cataloging in Publication Data

Christopher, Matthew F
  Glue fingers.

  SUMMARY: Reluctant to play football because he
stutters, Billy Joe's first game discloses that he has no
reason to fear ridicule.
  [1.   Football—Fiction.   2.   Speech—Disorders—Fic-
tion]   I.   Venable, Jim, illus.   II.   Title.
PZ7. C458G [Fic]   74-22419
ISBN 0-316-13939-4

Published simultaneously in Canada
by Little, Brown & Company (Canada) Limited

PRINTED IN THE UNITED STATES OF AMERICA

U. S. 1929915

to Tommy

A long time ago Billy Joe had made a promise to himself. He would not play football on any team as long as he stuttered. Stuttering embarrassed him, and he hated it when anyone else mentioned his problem. He would play — but only at home with his brothers, Joshua, Jimmy Ray and Mike.

He was thinking of that promise as he shook hands with Fred Davis. Mr. Davis, a tall man wearing a jacket with the letter A printed on the front of it, was coach of the Applejacks.

"Hi, Billy Joe," he said, smiling. "You have a nice big farm here."

"Th-thanks," said Billy Joe nervously.

Mr. Davis's smiled broadened. "Billy Joe, I've seen you play football with your brothers. You catch passes as if you've got glue on your fingers. Have you?"

Billy Joe grinned as he glanced around at his brothers. They were standing next to Mr. Davis on a carpet of fresh autumn leaves.

"N-no," he answered bashfully.

Conscious of his stuttering, he turned red.

"I would like to sign you up on my team," said Mr. Davis. "We play on Saturday morning against the Maroons. How about it?"

Billy Joe had his answer ready. "N-no, thanks," he said, shaking his head. "I'm-I'm not going to play football on-on any team."

He turned and started for the house, his heart beating like a drum.

"Billy Joe!" cried Jimmy Ray. "It's your big chance! You should play!"

Like Joshua and Mike, he was older than Billy Joe.

"I w-won't play!" Billy Joe flung angrily over his shoulder. "Don't you understand? I j-just won't!"

He ran up the creaky porch steps just as Mom came to the door. "Well, I was about to call you guys for dinner," she said, holding the door open for him. Then her eyes narrowed. "Billy Joe, what's wrong?"

"Nothing," he said. But his mind was racing. *The guys know why I don't want to play football on any team. They know I get nervous when I'm around strangers, and even guys I know. They know that is when I stutter the most.*

"Are you sure nothing happened out there, Billy Joe?" Mom asked as he sat down.

"I'm sure, Mom. D-don't worry about me. I'm all right."

When the other boys and Dad came in, she asked them what happened out there. Mike explained it all, and no one said any more, much to Billy Joe's relief.

After dinner they went out to continue their farm work. Except Mike. He and Dad went to the big red barn to repair the hay mower.

"Billy Joe," said Joshua, starting up the subject again, "you're crazy for letting your stuttering stop you from playing football."

Billy Joe's eyes snapped. "That's my b-business!" he cried.

"Boy!" said Joshua. "And they say mules are stubborn. You're more stubborn than any mule I've ever seen, Billy Joe!"

"You've got to forget how you talk, Billy Joe," Jimmy Ray broke in. "Take that chance to play football. It may never come again."

"If we were younger, *we* would!" Joshua exclaimed.

"You bet we would!" said Jimmy Ray. "Go 'head. Call up Mr. Davis, Billy Joe. Tell him you'll play."

Billy Joe clamped his teeth tightly together as he looked from one brother to the other. "Will you shut up?" he yelled, and scrambled out to the half-plowed field where he had left the tractor. He got up on it, started it, and shoved it into gear. Soon the smell of exhaust mixed with the sweet, fresh smell of the newly turned earth.

I would give anything to play football on a team! he wanted to shout at them. *But I can't! The guys would laugh me off the field!*

That night he couldn't fall asleep.
His mind kept churning and churning,
turning over what Joshua and Jimmy
Ray had said to him about playing
football. He realized he wouldn't have
to talk while he played. He could keep
as tight-mouthed as a clam.

Before he fell asleep he came to a
decision.

The next day he telephoned Mr. Davis. "Okay, Mr. Davis," he said. "I'll p-play."

"Fine, Billy Joe!" Mr. Davis replied happily. "I'll bring some papers over this evening for you and your father to sign."

Early that evening he came over, and Billy Joe and Dad signed papers. Later that evening Billy Joe was examined by Dr. Fuller, and passed. The next day after school Mr. Davis gave him a uniform, and he practiced with the Applejacks, most of the time running out for passes.

He attended school with most of the kids on the team. But he was no real friend with any of them. *Who would want a stuttering kid for a friend?* he always thought.

The morning of the game was chilly. Billy Joe, proud to be wearing a football uniform — but still scared, blew on his hands to keep them warm.

The Maroons kicked off. Larry Tucker, the Applejacks' safety man, caught the end-over-end kick and ran it to their thirty-eight-yard line.

In the huddle Timmy Hale, the Applejacks' quarterback, snapped an order. They broke out of the huddle, ran to the line of scrimmage, and Timmy started to bark signals: "Twenty-one! Twenty-eight! Thirteen!"

The ball snapped from the center. Timmy grabbed it, faded back, handed it to Larry. Larry plunged through the line for a three-yard gain.

The Applejacks lost two yards on the next play, however, on a run around right end. Third down, nine yards to go for a first down. The chances looked slim.

"Are you ready, Billy Joe?" asked Timmy in the huddle.

"R-ready," said Billy Joe nervously.

The signals. The snap. The pass.
Billy Joe saw the ball arching through
the air like an arrow as he raced down
the field. He reached for it. Just then a

Maroons player leaped for the ball and struck Billy Joe on the arm.

Billy Joe lost his balance and fell. Pounding his fist hard against the ground, he glared up at the player. "That's in-interference!" he shouted.

The Maroon said nothing, just looked at him and walked away. Then Billy Joe saw a flag lying on the ground, and a referee standing over it.

Timmy ran up, grinning. "We're in luck, Billy Joe!" he cried, helping Billy Joe to his feet. "The ref's spotting the ball where the guy bumped into you."

"What d-do you mean, l-luck?" echoed Billy Joe, frowning. "I might have run for a t-touchdown if he hadn't bumped into me."

Timmy smiled. "If you had caught it," he said. "And I don't think you would have. It was too far ahead of you."

"No! I'm sure I . . ." Billy Joe let the words die on his lips. He saw the other players looking at him, and his face got red.

How do you like that? he thought.

None of them think I would have caught it! They just don't want to say it!

Larry fumbled the ball on the next play, and the Maroons recovered it. In five plays they scored a touchdown, and passed successfully for the extra point. Maroons 7, Applejacks 0.

The Maroons scored again in the second quarter, then hit again on a pass for the extra point.

Billy Joe looked sadly at Coach Davis during halftime. *I'm doing nothing to help the team, Coach*, his look said plainly.

In the third quarter Larry ran twice
for a gain of eight yards, getting the
ball on the Maroons' twenty-one-yard
line. In the huddle, Billy Joe saw that
every guy was nervous and afraid that
the Applejacks were going down to
their first defeat of the season.

"T-Timmy," he said, "th-throw me a pass. A real long pass."

Timmy looked at him. "They have your number, Billy Joe," he said. "They have you covered like a tent."

"Try me," Billy Joe insisted.

Timmy looked at the other guys in the huddle as if to see what they thought of the idea.

"Do it," said Johnny Ruane, a halfback. "If he gets under it, he'll catch it. Larry and I will block for him."

"Okay," said Timmy. "Let's go!"

At the snap from center, Billy Joe took off as if he had been shot from a sling. Two Maroons chased after him, keeping close to his heels as Timmy heaved him a pass. It was a long one, all right, heading for the end zone. Neither Johnny nor Larry were close enough to block the Maroons.

But, suddenly, the gap between Billy Joe and the two Maroons widened as his legs seemed to sprout wings. He

practically flew across the goal line,
reached for the pass, and caught it on
the tips of his fingers! Touchdown!

The guys jumped on him, hugged him, slapped him on the back. "Man, you're all right, Billy Joe!" they cried.

Larry booted the extra point.

Maroons 14, Applejacks 7.

In the fourth quarter Johnny picked
up a Maroon fumble and raced for the
Applejacks' second touchdown. Larry's
kick for the extra point was no good,
and the Applejacks went almost crazy.

U. S. 1929915

With less than three minutes to play, the Maroons tried to run the ball, but failed to gain the ten yards they needed for a first down. The Applejacks took

over the ball. With fifty seconds left, Timmy heaved a pass to Billy Joe from his twenty-yard-line to the forty. Again Billy Joe ran as if wings were on his feet. He caught the ball, stumbled, kept his footing, and scampered all the way for a touchdown.

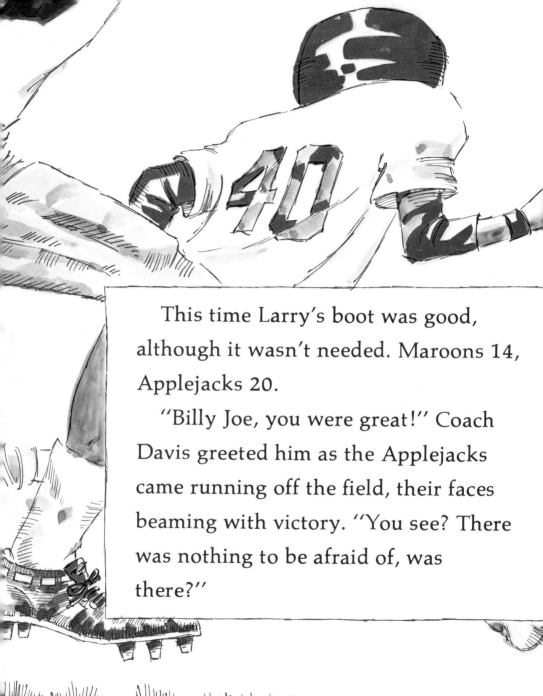

This time Larry's boot was good, although it wasn't needed. Maroons 14, Applejacks 20.

"Billy Joe, you were great!" Coach Davis greeted him as the Applejacks came running off the field, their faces beaming with victory. "You see? There was nothing to be afraid of, was there?"

Billy Joe wiped the sweat from his forehead and smiled. "No, Coach," he admitted. "N-no, there wasn't. That's because the guys are great, too. They didn't laugh at me. Th-they cheered me, instead."